Rabén & Sjögren Stockholm

Originally published in Sweden by Rabén & Sjögren
under the title *Kanin-Bad*
copyright © 1986 by Lena Anderson
All rights reserved
Library of Congress catalog card number: 89-063049
First American edition 1990
Printed in Italy

ISBN 91 29 59652 1

R & S Books are distributed in the United States of America
by Farrar, Straus and Giroux, New York;
in the United Kingdom by Ragged Bears, Andover;
in Canada by Vanwell Publishing, St.Catharines
and in Australia by ERA Publications, Adelaide

Lena Anderson

BUNNY
BATH

R&S
BOOKS

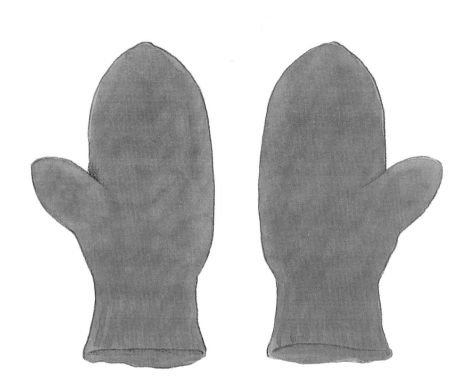